A Child's First Library of Values

The Heart of Winter

A Book about Helping People

A Child's First Library of Values

The
Heart
of Winter

Without thinking of herself, an old lady helps others in their time of need, and in return is rewarded with kindness and friendship. *The Heart of Winter* is just one of the international storybooks that make up *A Child's First Library of Values*, a series of delightful stories, beautiful illustrations and universal values.

The Heart of Winter

A Book about Helping People

TIME-LIFE KIDS

Once upon a time in Japan, there was a small teahouse by the side of a mountain path. The teahouse was owned by an old lady who lived there by herself.

Every day, the old lady made wonderful rice dumplings and all the travelers who passed by stopped to taste them.

"What delicious rice dumplings," they all said, before continuing their journeys, much refreshed.

In the wintertime, there was always snow in front of the teahouse. The old lady had a hard time clearing it all away.

Every day, she first had to remove the snow from around the shop, and then make her rice dumplings and prepare tea in order to get ready for her customers.

"This really is a hard task," muttered the old lady to herself, as she shoveled the snow. "My back is breaking."

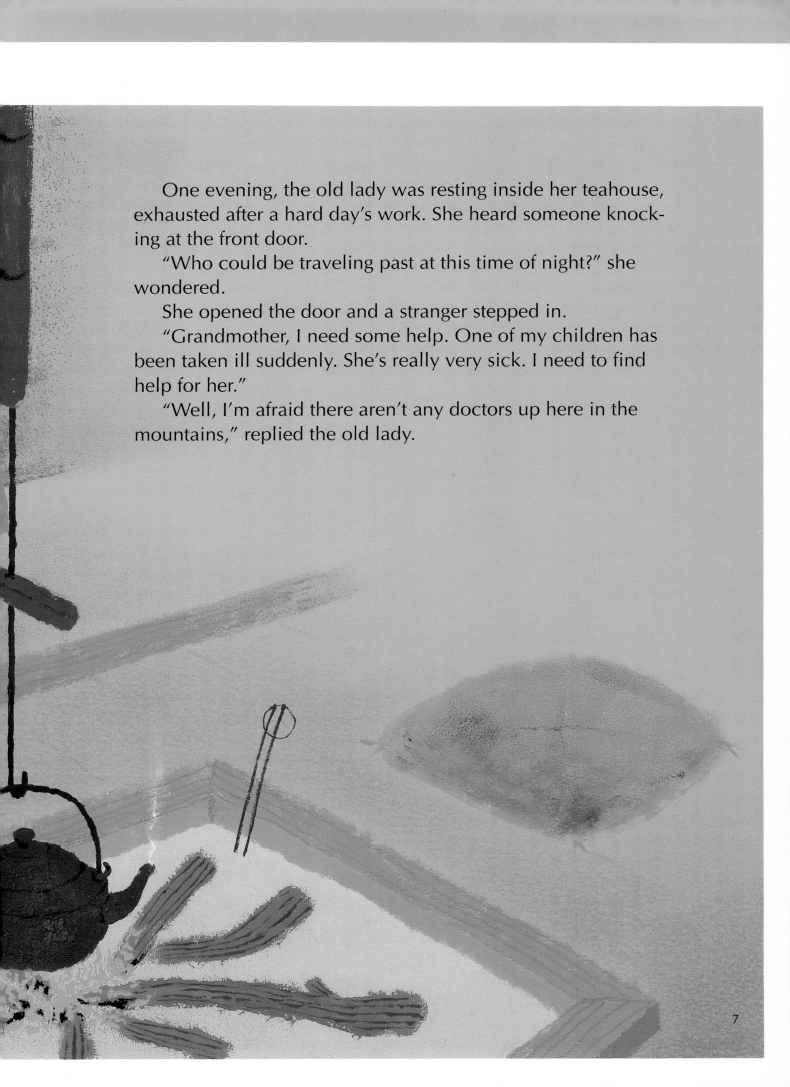

One evening, the old lady was resting inside her teahouse, exhausted after a hard day's work. She heard someone knocking at the front door.

"Who could be traveling past at this time of night?" she wondered.

She opened the door and a stranger stepped in.

"Grandmother, I need some help. One of my children has been taken ill suddenly. She's really very sick. I need to find help for her."

"Well, I'm afraid there aren't any doctors up here in the mountains," replied the old lady.

"I don't know what to do," said the man. "She's the youngest of my five children and she's got a high fever. She's become very weak."

"Have you given her any medicine yet?" asked the old lady.

"No, we don't have any to give her," replied the anxious man.

Hearing that, the old lady quickly fetched some homegrown herbal medicine and gave it to him.

"You should boil this and make her drink it. That will bring down the fever and make her well again. Why don't I come to your house and prepare it for her myself?"

"That's very kind of you," said the man. "We live high up in the mountains. Follow me."

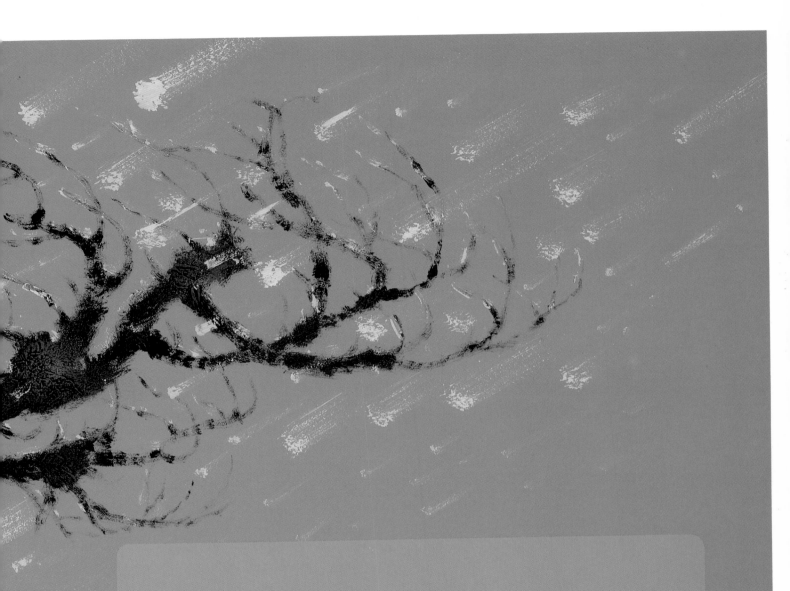

The old lady lit a lantern and the two set out together
into the stormy night. The wind soon blew out the lantern
and the old lady was afraid she would stumble and fall.

"I can't see where I'm going without the light," she said.

"Don't worry, Grandmother," said the man. "I'll carry
you."

He lifted her up and they made their way swiftly
through the snow. The old lady was surprised at how easily
he could find his way in the dark.

When they arrived at the man's house, the old lady found the sick child moaning in pain. Her three brothers and her sister looked on anxiously.

The old lady prepared her herbal medicine at once.

"Drink this and you'll soon feel better," she told the child.

She sat with the sick child all night long, giving her medicine and soothing her hot forehead with a cool, damp cloth.

By the next morning, the fever had passed and the young girl was sleeping comfortably.

"You have done us a big favor," said the man, and he and his wife bowed respectfully to the old lady to express their gratitude.

"We are very poor but we would like to give you something in return for your help."

But the kindhearted old lady refused to accept any gift.

"Don't mention it," she said. "I'm just happy that your child is getting better."

"Well, we will never forget your kindness to us," they said.

The four children offered to walk the old lady back to her home. It was a beautiful morning. The snow had stopped falling and the sky was clear.

The children set out in high spirits, flattening the crisp fresh snow with their feet in order to make the journey easier for the old lady.

"Come this way, Grandmother," they called. "We want to show you something beautiful."

The children led the old lady to the edge of a frozen lake. The morning sun was shining brightly and the ice-covered lake was as clear as a mirror. The beauty of the ice and snow was reflected in the wide surface of the lake.

The old lady stood there silently, full of admiration for the breathtaking sight.

The tall trees at the edge of the lake were dusted with snow. Long, thin icicles hung from the tips of some of their branches.

In the silvery light of the sun, the trees appeared to be covered with flowers of ice.

"What a magical sight," thought the old lady.

When they reached the old lady's teahouse, the children said goodbye.

"Take care," said the kind old lady, as she watched them leave.

As they turned to go, she spotted something strange. The children all had bushy brown tails peeping out of their clothes.

She looked closer.

"Why, they're little foxes!" she exclaimed.

The old lady sat by the fire and made herself some tea while she thought about what had happened.

"So, they were all foxes," she thought. "The father fox disguised himself as a man and came to me because his child was sick. They deceived me."

She poured herself more tea.

"Well, it doesn't matter anyway. Being sick is as bad for an animal as it is for a person. I'm glad that I was able to help her."

Not long afterwards, there was a spell of bad weather. It snowed all day, every day. The old lady's teahouse was almost buried under the snow and there was too much of it for her to clear away herself.

"Oh dear, my house will collapse under the weight of all this snow if I don't do something," she sighed. Suddenly she heard the sound of singing nearby.

The old lady opened her door and looked out. To her surprise, she saw two large foxes and five little foxes shoveling snow from her roof and the path outside her house.

The foxes sang merrily as they shoveled the snow out of the way.

The old lady realized it was the fox family she had helped earlier in the winter. They had come to return her favor.

After the work was finished, the old lady invited the fox family into her house for some tea and rice dumplings.

"Thank you for all your help today," she said.

"Not at all," said the fox couple. "We simply wanted to return your kindness to us."

The five little foxes were having a good time.

"Your rice dumplings are delicious," they told her mischievously. "We'll always be pleased to come and clear your snow."

The fire in the stove burned brightly. The old lady poured more tea and sighed contentedly.

What the story tells us. . .

As parents, we are always seeking ways to reinforce life's important lessons with our children. *A Child's First Library of Values* offers an opportunity for doing so in the context of wonderful, entertaining stories. You may choose to use these books as a springboard for further discussion. The following is a list of universal values reflected in this volume.

- **Helping others.** The kindhearted teahouse owner is eager to help others—when the man comes to her door one night asking for help, she gives him medicine for his sick child and goes out into the cold night to help care for the girl. When people do things for each other, even if it means making sacrifices, it makes everyone feel good.

- **Working hard.** The woman in the story puts a lot of effort into preparing refreshments for the travelers who stop at her teahouse. Hard work provides satisfaction and pride in a job well done and generates respect and admiration from others.

- **Showing gratitude.** The fox couple express their gratitude to the woman for saving their daughter and she thanks the foxes for clearing her snow. Thanking someone for a gift or a favor demonstrates respect and appreciation for the efforts of others.

- **Doing good for the sake of doing good.** Some people expect a reward in return for doing a favor, but others know that just doing the right thing can be satisfaction enough. The story shows that generosity is often rewarded with kindness and friendship, which are far more valuable than material rewards.

- **Returning kindness.** When people are kind to each other, they spread happiness. The fox family returns the woman's favor when the opportunity arises, which allows them to share that good feeling with her.

- **Appreciating nature.** Taking time to admire a beautiful sight or enjoy a glorious day, as the young foxes encourage the woman to do, provides a way to stay in touch with the world's natural beauty and serves as a gentle reminder of the need to look after the environment.

- **Showing forgiveness.** Even after the woman realizes that she has been deceived, she understands why the father fox disguised himself to get her help. Knowing why other people are sometimes less than honest can help in finding ways to forgive them.

A Child's First Library of Values

The Heart of Winter

Authorized English-language edition published by:
Time Life Asia
VP Time Life International,
*   Regional Director, Asia*
*   and Latin America:*   Trevor E. Lunn
CFO and General Manager: Deepak Desai
Production Manager: Tommy K. Ng
Editorial and New Product
*   Development Manager:*   Kate Nussey
Editor: Vikki Weston
Translation from Chinese: Cathy Poon

First printing 1997. Reprinted 1998.
Printed in Hong Kong.

Time Life Asia is a division of Time Life Inc.

ISBN 0-7835-1311-9

Authorized English-language edition
© 1997 Time Life Inc.

Translated from the Chinese-language edition
© 1995 Time Life Inc.
Original Japanese-language edition published by:
Gakken Co. Ltd., Tokyo, Japan
© 1988 Gakken Co. Ltd.

Original story by Eiko Takeda and illustration by
Kozo Shimizu.
Eiko Takeda was born in Tokyo, Japan, in 1930.
She is a writer of illustrated storybooks and a
journalist.
Kozo Shimizu was born in Fukui Prefecture,
Japan, in 1935. He is a storybook writer and
illustrator.